the First GayPride Parade

June 28, 1970

the Birth of WorldPride

Homosexual
Love and Equality

Jeri Lee

the First Gay Pride Parade

June 28, 1970

the Birth of WorldPride

Artist Author Jeri Lee

ISBN: 978-0-692-68452-8

About the Author
Jeri Lee

Jeri was born in 1939 on a small farm in northern Maine and realized from an early age the real value in life was living it, and the most significant asset was a fact, not faith.

Although the dollar is an idea exchanged for value, it cannot purchase the magic of life, higher awareness, and contact with cosmic consciousness.

This knowing is embedded in your DNA and is a universal gift that lets you recognize that part of you that reads the akashic records.

Jeri walked through the halls and rooms of our educational system, realizing it did not teach you how to think but instead what to think.

She collected her Wisdom from the facts she saw written on the walls. She later realized that not everyone could see this; if they could see, they could not read. Then if they could read, many could not understand. In the '70s, Jeri met the hand that wrote upon her wall, and when she asked his name, he responded, "I have none, but you may call me OM, and I am your spirit guide." Om was an impressive ally with his massive height and three blue eyes.

IN MEMORY OF KATHLEEN INEZ LEE
SEPT. 25, 1937   SEPT. 28, 1991

An epitaph to "MY THEE",
Great lady Kathy Lee -
Thank you for being you
   and letting me be me.
You gave so much then,
   took the same to give
   and give again.
You will be missed so very much
   by every soul you touched;
Cradled deep within our hearts
   you planted the seed of love -
We'll nourish it with loving tears
   in the caves of our loneness,
That it may blossom for all to see
   the reflection of your image.
I know you found that perfect peace
   in the light at the end of the trail -
Total nothingness.
Now pause,
Now rest,
Then begin once again your cycle
   of happiness.

"YOUR THEE"

Kathleen Lee
and Ali

1970 The Gay Community - The first Christopher Street West gay pride parade is held honoring the rebellion at the Stonewall Inn in New York the preceding year. Rev. Troy Perry, Bob Humphries, and a lesbian on horseback led the parade from its starting point at McCadden Place and Hollywood Boulevard.

The First GayPride Parade by Jeri Lee

"Out of the Closets and into the Streets"

"We're HERE
We're QUEER,
and
We Won't be SILENT!"

Acknowledgments

My thanks to the photographers who took all the photos I found on the internet and used in my book. There is limited information on this historical event, and I hope I have added to its current history. If, in the process, I wrongly shared your photo, then please forgive me. I was there, and you were there. So with that logic, we shared the event. However, you recorded it, and I was too busy being a part of it.
I browsed through Wikipedia, One, the Advocate, YouTube, and more for details I might need to include or remember.
I am 86 and remember the day and time quite well, but this old brain needs to shake the cobwebs off the memories to write this book, so I need all the help I can get. I hope I have done justice to what we share.
Jeri Lee

I printed the proto-type of this book in November of 2024, and it is now the second week of January 2025. I am sitting in front of my stove, watching the blaze of the wood fire that keeps me warm from fall to spring. Ironically, the screen on my wall shows the same Element greedily devouring the setting of my book. I now live in a wooded canyon of Mo, and last night, nature gifted us with 6 inches of snow, while my Los Angeles and Hollywood memories go up in flames and get buried in Ashes. I have witnessed the Rath of those Santa Anna winds from Temple City to Wrightwood. Now watching the Hollywood hills dance like torches from Dante's Inferno, I remember my fear as I drove down Cajon Pass at dusk with winds whipping the flames on both sides of the highway. As the flames flickers and the smoke dies, may our future not be rewritten by the history: "Nero fiddled while Rome burned" vs. "Trump gloated as California burned".

As I edit the proofs and add final details to this book of my memories, how can I possibly comprehend the effect this disaster could and will have on the advancement of Pride in the city of Los Angeles? As the Gay community, CSW, put Los Angeles on the global map, they, in turn, turned us into their most significant industry, competing with Hollywood. Lets us remember that this disaster not only destroyed physical structures, it crippled, handicapped, and confused the future of the growth of PRIDE. My Generation of Homosexuals are the ashes that laid the bedrock of today's Global Pride Accomplishments. May we be appreciated..

Los Angeles, California, hosted the world's first officially permitted LGBTQ+ Pride parade on June 28, 1970.

The parade, originally called the Gay Pride Parade, took place on Hollywood Boulevard and was a significant milestone in the fight for LGBTQ+ rights.

The event followed the Stonewall Uprising in New York City in 1969, which sparked the modern LGBTQ+ rights movement.

The Los Angeles parade was a pivotal moment, as it was the first time a large-scale LGBTQ+ demonstration was openly permitted and celebrated.

The parade featured floats, protest signs, costumes, and music, showcasing the growing visibility and activism of the LGBTQ+ community. The event was a significant step forward for LGBTQ+ rights and helped pave the way for future Pride parades and celebrations around the world.

Other cities: Similar Demonstrations were also held in New York and Chicago on the same day. However, Los Angeles was the only Parade with a Legal Permit.

A "march" is typically a form of protest where people walk together to express a political viewpoint or advocate for change, while a "demonstration" is a broader term encompassing any public gathering to show support or opposition to something, and a "parade" is a procession of people usually organized for celebration, often with festive elements like costumes and floats, with the primary purpose being to mark a special occasion rather than protest.

There isn't much information about a video of the first Los Angeles Gay Pride Parade in 1970, but here's some information about the parade itself:

The first permitted Gay Pride Parade in Los Angeles was held on June 28, 1970, and took place on Hollywood Boulevard.

The parade was held on the one-year anniversary of the Stonewall Uprising, a riot that began when the police raided a gay bar in Manhattan.

Thousands of LGBT+ people gathered in Los Angeles and other cities to demonstrate for equal rights and commemorate Stonewall.

The one-day celebrations eventually evolved into a full month of LGBTQ pride, which became official in 1999 with a proclamation from former President Bill Clinton.

Wickapedia Says:

The West Coast of the United States saw a march in San Francisco on June 27, 1970, and 'Gay-in' on June 28, 1970, and a march in Los Angeles on June 28, 1970. In Los Angeles, Morris Kight (Gay Liberation Front LA founder), Reverend Troy Perry (Universal Fellowship of Metropolitan Community Churches founder) and Reverend Bob Humphries (United States Mission founder) gathered to plan a commemoration. They settled on a parade down Hollywood Boulevard. But securing a permit from the city was no easy task. They named their organization Christopher Street West, "as ambiguous as we could be."] But Rev. Perry recalled the Los Angeles Police Chief Edward M. Davis telling him, "As far as I'm concerned, granting a permit to a group of homosexuals to parade down Hollywood Boulevard would be the same as giving a permit to a group of thieves and robbers." Grudgingly, the Police Commission granted the permit, though there were fees exceeding $1.5 million. After the American Civil Liberties Union stepped in, the commission dropped all its requirements but a $1,500 fee for police service. That, too, was dismissed when the California Superior Court ordered the police to provide protection as they would for any other group. The eleventh-hour California Supreme Court decision ordered the police commissioner to issue a parade permit citing the "constitutional guarantee of freedom of expression." From the beginning, L.A. parade organizers and participants knew there were risks of violence. Kight received death threats right up to the morning of the parade. Unlike later editions, the first gay parade was very quiet. The marchers convened on Mccadden Place in Hollywood, marched north and turned east onto Hollywood Boulevard.The Advocate reported "Over 1,000 homosexuals and their friends staged, not just a protest march, but a full-blown parade down world-famous Hollywood Boulevard."

With more than 400,000 people descending upon 1.9 square miles, Los Angeles Pride is the largest gathering of LGBT people and allies in Southern California. The parade, which has long been the centerpiece of Pride weekend, was the first of its kind in the world when it began in 1970.

It was fast approaching one year since the Stonewall riots of June, 1969, when Reverend Bob Humphries (United States Mission founder), Morris Kight (Gay Liberation Front founder) and Reverend Troy Perry (Universal Fellowship of Metropolitan Community Churches founder) gathered to plan a commemoration. They settled on a parade down Hollywood Boulevard. But homosexuality was still illegal in the state of California at the time, so securing a permit from the city was no easy task.

Rev. Perry recalled the Los Angeles Police Chief Edward M. Davis telling him, "As far as I'm concerned, granting a permit to a group of homosexuals to parade down Hollywood Boulevard would be the same as giving a permit to a group of thieves and robbers." Grudgingly, the Police Commission granted the permit, though there were fees exceeding $1.5 million. After the American Civil Liberties Union stepped in, the commission dropped all its requirements but a $1,500 fee for police service. That, too, was dismissed when the California Superior Court ordered the police to provide protection as they would for any other group.

All that negotiation left the team with only two days to throw together a parade before the June 28th anniversary. In other cities, the anniversary was marked with marches, rallies, and demonstrations, but in Los Angeles, the parade was the display of Pride, complete with a float from The Advocate magazine, loaded with men in swimsuits, and a conservative gay group clad in business suits. Soon, there was talk of making it an annual event. It would become the model for Pride celebrations across the nation.

Wickapedia

Los Angeles' First Gay Pride Parade
Trailed New York's by Hours

Chris Nichols June 10 2024
1975 Gay Pride Parade on Hollywood Boulevard
SCMFT/HollywoodPhotographs.com

Although Los Angeles was home to the first gay rights organization, the first LGBT church, the first gay and lesbian magazines, the first gay motorcycle club (which is still rolling today!) and many other milestones of LGBT history, New York is actually the first city to hold a gay pride parade — in fact, it was held just a few hours before ours.

L.A.'s first permitted parade rolled down Hollywood Boulevard on June 28, 1970. It was led by the Christopher Street West Association, which today produces the big downtown L.A. Pride music festival. To commemorate the first anniversary of the Stonewall riots, organizations on both coasts planned parades on the same day; Greenwich Village at noon and Hollywood at dusk. Twelve hundred revelers including drag queens, a lesbian on horseback and a giant python marched in the L.A.'s first sanctioned and permitted pride event. The Los Angeles Police Department reported 4,000 bystanders on that first outing, while organizers put the number closer to 30,000.

We might have started a little late that day, but some folks argue that the first "parade" was an organized caravan of cars objecting to the exclusion of gays from the military in May 1966. Protest marches were held around the country, but L.A.'s car culture had a motorcade of vehicles with dishwasher-sized box signs on their roofs cruising through the Fairfax district. A few months later, sympathetic crowds gathered outside the Black Cat bar in Silver Lake to protest police brutality there.

While the bicoastal time difference cost us the 1970 parade title, there is no doubt that L.A. had already been at the forefront of the gay rights movement for two decades

New York

In June, in New York City, to commemorate the 1969 spontaneous demonstrations on Christopher Street, this demonstration be called CHRISTOPHER STREET LIBERATION DAY."

The Stonewall Inn is located on Christopher Street and was the origin point for the Uprising. From the outset, organizers envisioned it as a national celebration, "We also propose that we contact Homophile organizations throughout the country and suggest that they hold parallel demonstrations on that day. We propose a nationwide show of support."

Thus, in Los Angeles, California, CSW, " CHRISTOPHER STREET WEST," was organized as the West Coast competition.

50+ Years of Pride Library of Congress.

Since June 1970, LGBTQ+ people have continued to gather together in June to march with Pride. Learn more about the pioneering gay rights activists who created Pride by exploring the LGBTQ+ Collections at the Library of Congress.

Have a question about LGBTQ+ history? Get in touch with Library of Congress Librarians and subject experts using our Ask a Librarian service. Also, be sure to take a look at LGBTQ+ Studies: A Resource Guide and read the blog post Pride at 50: From Stonewall to Today.

Take a look at Library Digital Collections related to LGBTQ+ studies, history and culture:

LGBTQ+ Studies Web Archive Collection

The Library of Congress Pride Portal

Speaking Out: LGBT Veterans

Long Live

WorldPride

The First GayPride Parade by Jeri Lee C.Ht.

June 28, 1970

I am finally telling my story, a narrative woven through the vibrant tapestry of Los Angeles's LGB history. Born in 1939, I grew up in a time when being different was met with hostility and cruelty. Being Gay before 1970 and publicly exposing that you were homosexual was to admit you were insane, perverse, deviant, and evil, to say the least. Believe me, I know. I am 86 and finally decided it was "do or die time." Although this might be a small piece of Los Angeles's gay history, it is, in my opinion, an important one, and it was not documented by a data-collecting organization that I could find in today's expansive database.

That prompted me to finally "Come Out" and expose the mystery of who the 'Lesbian on Horseback' was in the statement often found that reads, "Rev. Troy Perry, Bob Humphries, and a lesbian on horseback led the parade from its starting point at McCadden Place and Hollywood Boulevard. I have often wondered if the Homosexual community ever wondered who that unknown Lesbian on horseback was and the identity of the buckskin she sat on. Perhaps much in the same way, respectful Americans questioned the identity of the unknown soldier in Arlington National Cemetery.

.   The First LA Gay Parade on June 28, 1970, in Los Angeles was Led by a beautiful Palomino Gelding Named Ali. Sitting on his back as the leader of this parade was a Lesbian named Kathleen Lee.

The First GayPride Parade by Jeri Lee

She was my loving wife, and Ali was our proud asset. I lived it, I was there, and I know it is a fact. At that time in our space, Kathy and I were married by a church-ordained minister. Our marriage was not recognized by the law, it was discriminated against by Society and objected by family. I changed my name to Lee so we could live together as sisters without being obvious, as long as we showed no closeness in public.

Sunday afternoon, June 28, 1970, was 73 degrees in Los Angeles and a perfect day for a parade, so why not celebrate this Giant win for equal rights for the future generations of homosexuals in the world?

That One Big Step for LGBT was off the corner of Hollywood Boulevard and McCadden Place. Today, at that corner, a bronze plaque says, "Christopher Street West. On June 28, 1970, the first Gay Pride parade in Los Angeles stepped off from this corner.

By our current standards, it was small in size. About 2,000 people showed up to march, drive their floats, and walk their pets, and probably an equal number cheered from the sidewalks. With all due consideration, it was Great, considering the permit was not granted until the day before the event.

The First GayPride Parade by Jeri Lee C.Ht.

Kathy was dressed like an Indian in a brown leather vest with fringes and tall matching handmade boots. She was seated bareback on her buckskin Ali and led the First Gay parade. Directly behind the lesbian on horseback was a float by The Society of Anubis, of which Kathy Lee was a founding member.

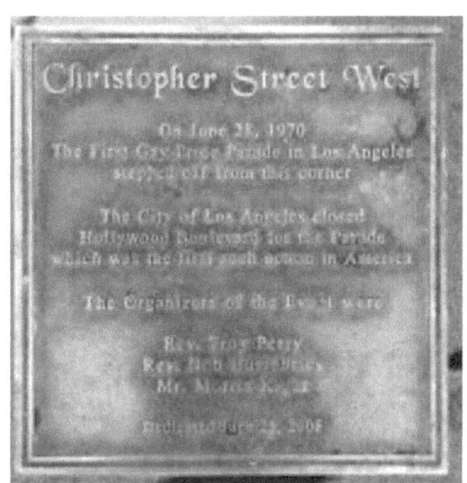

Anubis was a Private Gay Club that sheltered members from the brutal abuse of gays by the police. Being a member of the first float could have been why Kathy and Ali led the parade. Then came the float by The Advocate, The leading publication on Gay, Lesbian, Bisexual, Transgender, Queer News and Politics. Followed by a barefoot Gay light stepper wearing only his briefs and a smile while patting an active giant snake.

They were followed by many marchers carrying handmade flags and banners that proclaimed the conditions of the closets they lived in. Some demanded God-given freedoms as our birthright, while others waved outcries from the legal side of our challenge.

Without a band, Willie Smith drove his minibus as a music box, and the crowds applauded.

There is limited information available on the exact details of that first celebration except for those of us brave enough to attend and even braver to participate in the parade.

How the first Gay Parade got its Permit

We Celebrate Gay Pride today and take it for granted that it has always been a special day for the homosexual community. That is far from a fact, and I am one of a few living Lesbians who know the facts, instead of reading them. Now, the young Gays party and march in the streets with social acceptance and most likely never think or care about the pioneers that gave them that right. How they endured the social, emotional. and mental abuse in the writing of that chapter of Gay life and History.

With protests, marches, and rebellions, we approached the possibility of legally getting a parade permit, but that was not as easy as it sounded and almost did not happen.

The Los Angeles Police Commission issued parade permits and imposed severe financial and other conditions on the pride parade organizers that other groups didn't have to meet. The commissioners, as well as the police dept, were not only openly hostile to the parade organizers, but they were brutal to members of the homosexual community;

I know this as a fact. One night in the 1970's I was waiting at the rear door of a Pasadena Lesbian bar for Kathy and she mistakenly went out the front door. She was arested by a Pasadena Police officer for no reason except being in a lesbian bar. He took her to the police office, handcuffed to a chair, and pistol-whipped her. Having no grounds to book her, after several hours of toucher, he dumped her on the street. She was wounded and bloody when I found her the following morning after searching all night. This is a true story, and unfortunately, it happened often by the brutal police officers as their personal entertainment.

The First GayPride Parade by Jeri Lee C.Ht.

How the first Gay Parade got its Permit

Homosexuality was illegal at the time, so the Police Chief Edward M. Davis just mocked them for applying for a parade permit. He remarked, as far as I'm concerned, granting a permit to a group of homosexuals to parade down Hollywood Boulevard would be the same as giving a permit to a group of thieves and robbers.

That was when MY FRIENDS Rev. Bob Humphries, of the United States Mission founder, Morris Kight, Gay Liberation Front founder, and Rev. Troy Perry, Universal Fellowship of Metropolitan Community Churches founder, gathered to plan a commemoration. They settled on a parade down Hollywood Boulevard. But securing a permit from the city took a lot of work.

The Police Commission Grudgingly granted the permit, though fees were exceeding $1.5 million. Of course, that was ridiculous and rejected by the three leading organizers of the event. After the American Civil Liberties Union stepped in, the commission dropped all its requirements but a $1,500 fee for police service. That, too, was dismissed when the California Superior Court ordered the police to protect as they would for any other group.

Rev Troy Perry admitted that they minimized the word Homosexuality by using his church name, "Metropolitan Community Church," on the permit. They did not mention that MCC was for LGB and when Rev Troy was asked what kind of a church it was, his answer was, "a Christian One."

All that negotiation left the team with only two days to organize a parade before the June 28th anniversary of Christopher Street N.Y. and the creation of Christopher Street West.

In other Cities across the country, this day was marked with marches, rallies, and demonstrations. In Los Angeles, the FIRST GAY PARADE became the seed of the PRIDE movement.

The First GayPride Parade by Jeri Lee.

How the first Gay Parade got its Permit

Hundreds marched down Hollywood Boulevard in the nation's first legally permitted gay pride parade. I am proud to say we were there, and my wife, Kathy, with our pet, Ali, proudly led that national event.

There were men bedecked in fairy wings. Go-go dancers on a flatbed truck. A young man with an Alaskan husky and a sign that read "We Don't All Walk Poodles" in the pet-walking section. The Gay Liberation Front of Los Angeles came down the boulevard carrying banners and shouting, "Two, four, six, eight...gay is just as good as being straight."

The Metropolitan Community Church choir in flowing robes singing "Onward Christian Soldiers."

The First GayPride Parade by Jeri Lee C.Ht.

The Society of Anubis

The Society of Anubis was a lesbian and gay organization founded in 1967 as a semi-secret Gay society in the L.A. area. Its original purpose was to show the public an accurate picture of homosexuals and that they are worthwhile members of Society. In comparison to other similar organizations at the time, it was conservative with an open approach to homosexuality. It was named for the Egyptian god Anubis's for his healing powers and fairness in weighing the feather on the scale of balance and equality.

This Society received a charter from the state of Ca. in 1969. With Helen Niehaus as their president, they supported legislation to enact just and enlightened sex laws. With approximately 800 members and growing fast, it represented both gays and lesbians equally. They were chartered as a nonprofit organization to promote their political goal.

Society has increased from its early start, and its outreach has resulted in the successful acceptance of new legislation.

The Society maintained a ten-acre ranch and a club in the San Gabriel Valley for a more private gathering as a substitute for the local gay bars.

While focusing on social and community programs, the Society was influenced by the radical character of gay and lesbian organizing at the time. Because of exposure, the Society became more political involved, as its membership was encouraged to vote with their gay and lesbian status in mind. Then, on the evening of January 11, 1970, members of the Society took part in a Gay Rights demonstration in Los Angeles. The purpose was to protest against laws making homosexual acts between adults legally a felony and putting pressure on the California Supreme Court to grant a hearing for equal rights given to everyone. At this event 300 protesters marched along Hollywood Blvd supporting flags, signs, and banners.

The society played a large part in the orgazination of the first gay parade in L.A. on June 28, 1970. They took their rightful position as the first float in the parade lineup, placing my wife Kathleen Lee on her horse Ali to lead the historical event.

The First GayPride Parade   by Jeri Lee

Then came the Advocate's float

TThe second float in the line was that of the Advocate. It was one of the oldest LGB Magazines and is today the largest by adding LGBTQ to its program and prospering in the growth of the Homosexual community, which they played a significant part in successfully advancing.

It is available by subscription, printed bi-monthly, and is complete with a website. Both focus on news, politics, opinion, and arts and entertainment of interest to lesbians, gay men, bisexuals, transgender, and queer LGBTQ community.

They were established in 1967 as the first of its kind and played an impressive role in advancing the first LA Gay Parade. The paper was first published as a local newsletter by the activist group Personal Rights in Defense and Education, initialing the word 'PRIDE.' The Advocate newsletter was inspired by a police rade on a local LA bar named the Black Cat Tavern, on January 1, 1967. Its purpose was to be a connecting link of communication among its members as a group protection against the ongoing brutality of its members by the LA police dept.

Their size increased rapidly, and their web of necessity grew, and so did they until they became and still are the largest of their kind. During the heart of the Aids epidemic, they were instrumental in disseminating progressive information.

The Advocate was just a man's paper, catering to the man's man and homosexual sex entertainment. In 1992, they created a lesbian version to satisfy the needs and wants of the female side of Gay.

As part of the first LA Gay Parade, they laid claim to their rightful inheritance of the gains and glory of CSW PRIDE.

The First GayPride Parade by Jeri Lee

Most floats were local bars, bathhouses, or club advertisements with complementary colorful drag queens. One such float presented a Giant jar of Vaseline as its sexual theme.

Oh, wow.

Several convertibles chauffeured the honorary community members while most participants proudly marched. They are modeling their latest fashion, or lack thereof, or walking their favorite pet.

The Flags, Banners, and objects they carried pushed or pulled varied in intensity as to why they chose that slogan and words to amplify it.

Their effects echo in today's environment as accomplishments. Although the permit for the

parade did not give us the right to show affection in public, it offered a window of hope in our closet door. Today's Gay generation is much different because they do not have a closet to escape from, so they did not learn the lessons that made their predecessor heroes.

The First GayPride Parade by Jeri Lee

That first parade was a test for each member of the Gay community as to whether you have what it takes to stand up and be counted. Because it was illegal to be homosexual, and by marching in this first parade, you could be arrested or lose your job. It was a life of open denial for many closeted gays at the time.

The First GayPride Parade by Jeri Lee

The first Gay L.A. parable might have been small in size, but it was mighty in power as it exploded through the years.

June 28,1970
The First L.A.
GAY Parade

The First GayPride Parade by Jeri Lee

"Before Stonewall, we had the Daughters of Bilitis.

Today's Gay community is more diverse as its efforts have attracted numerous sexual issues outside of homosexuality. We marched in the LA streets for the rights of Homosexuals to Love each other and live everyday lives. It has developed into an attraction for all sex-oriented issues that deviate from the clinical sex behavior prescribed by the Vatican. Our label has grown from LGB to LGBTQ. Where does it go from here?

The First GayPride Parade by Jeri Lee

The first gay parade in Los Angeles was not merely a celebration; it was a critical moment of activism that set the stage for future movements.

The impact of this event reverberated through the years, influencing subsequent pride events and contributing to the growing visibility of LGBTQ+ issues in politics and society. Participants of the 1970 parade became trailblazers, paving the way for future generations to embrace their identities proudly. As we reflect on this historic event, it is essential to recognize its role in the broader struggle for LGBTQ+ rights, as well as the ongoing need for activism and advocacy in the face of continuing challenges.

The First GayPride Parade by Jeri Lee

The purpose was to protest against laws making homosexual acts between adults legally a felony and putting pressure on the California Supreme Court to grant a hearing for equal rights as granted to everyone by the U.S. Constitution.

The First GayPride Parade by Jeri Lee

On June 28th, 1969, a police raid on the N.Y. Stonewall Inn on Christopher Street incited six days of protests as homosexuals, Gay queens, and activists took to the streets. In the years leading up to the Stonewall Rebellion, resistance to police surveillance and violence, led primarily by queers and trans and people of color, was gaining momentum across the country. In Los Angeles, protests at Cooper's Donuts, The Black Cat in Silverlake, and The Patch in Wilmington reveal a growing L.A. local movement. The turn of the decade signaled a shift from the social acceptance efforts of the homophile movement to gay liberation. Influenced by the Civil Rights Movement, organizers sought to cultivate a queer political consciousness, provide social services, and take direct action.

The First GayPride Parade by Jeri Lee

.

The choice of the Boulevard for the 1970 march was a strategic one. By the 1920s, the film industry had put Hollywood on the global map. Over the next few decades, the neighborhood cultivated the rise of radio, television, and record industries, becoming a hub of nightlife and entertainment for culture makers. While by the 1950s, tourism was the primary industry, the image of the Boulevard became solidified in national memory. "It's a world-famous street," said founding member of the Los Angeles GLF chapter Morris Kight in 1970. "We wanted to be where the people were, where the media were, where the action was."

The First GayPride Parade by Jeri Lee

·

L.A. Gay Fairs Before CSW

Before CSW, Pioneer Days was a festival held in selected empty lots in the LA area. These carnivals were hosted by the Valley Business Alliance, an organization formed for gay and lesbian businesses and professionals. These festivals eventually evolved into today's Los Angeles LGBTQ Chamber of Commerce and the Pride Festival, which accompanies the gay parade.

The Valley Business Alliance was a group of very influential Gay men that I called my friends from early before the first gay LA parade. They were the Giants in the early Homoaexul scene in LA and the heart of all the major organizations and accomplishments at that time. They were Morris Kight, Troy Perry, Bob Humpties, and Pat Rocco.

Kathy and I participated in their functions by entering a booth for our jewelry in most shows they sponsored, whether a Gay street show or a gay rodeo. Of course, as part of the show, my teenage son played a significant role in bringing their attention to our booth.

The First GayPride Parade by Jeri Lee

L.A. Gay Fairs Before CSW

The Alliance would rent an empty lot, usually on some side street in a suburb of LA near their Studio City headquarters. It was typically sizeable and in a parking lot. Then, a chainlink fence around the area would be erected, creating a gated function to protect the attendants.

There would be a live band and a dancing area with a booth selling beer and other food. In addition, there would be booths for business. The primary reason for such a party was to create public awareness that we were ready for exposure. This did not sit well with the local churches who marched in front of our gate with banners saying typical hostile slogans while shouting turn or burn. The young males in these groups would often climb over the rear fence and attempt to beat up on the guys, calling them fagates. We policed the festival well because the L.A Police Dept. was part of the protesters. It never turned into a Stonewall.

By participating in these events, I got to meet and know the leading gay figures of the time, and you never knew what Hollywood celebrities would pass by.

The First GayPride Parade by Jeri Lee

L.A. Gay Fairs Before CSW

This is how I got to know a noteworthy lesbian who participated in the Pioneer Days Festivals: Ivy Bottiini and her life partner Dottie Wine. At one event, their T-shirt booth was next to mine, enabling us to protect the others back from those nasty little street kids who would steal anything they could get their dirty little hands on.

I first saw Ivy at the LGB center, where she performed on stage. That was the best humor I had witnessed as she performed a silent mime instructing you on "how to install your first tampon."

Ivy is one of the national heroes in the lesbian world, as she has been involved in NOW and in front of almost every major lesbian organization since those early days. She is well known for her paintings; they are as big and beautiful as she was.

She toured the country for several years performing "The Many Faces of Woman," a lesbian feminist one-woman show, and was director of the women's program at the Los Angeles Gay and Lesbian Community Services Center.

She was undoubtedly a champion of LGBT rights and died in 2021 at the age of 94.

The First GayPride Parade by Jeri Lee

L.A. Gay Fairs Before CSW

After the first LA gay parade in 1970, there was another in 1971 and another in 1972, but not in 1973. In 1974, a Valley Bussiness Alliance member, Pat Rocco, who had experience producing festivals along with Morris, Troy, and Pat, came up with the idea of a festival accompanying the parade.

The combination happened, and in 1974, the first festival was the offspring of the Pioneer Days celebrations. It was inlarged to include rides, games, food, and information booths, and Kathy and I were the first and only Artist booth. We registered with our business name, Shims Creative Workshop. The first Festival occurred in a parking lot at Sunset Boulevard and Cherokee.

The LA Police Dept was always hostile, and in 1979, CSW moved both the Parade and the Festival West to what would later become West Hollywood.

Of course, Kathy and I were always there as it grew to encompass giant fireworks as a climax. For 21 continuous years, we had a booth at LA Gay Festivals, along with Long Beach and San Francisco. 1991 was our last appearance because, on Sept 29, 1991, the angel of death stole her from me, and like an Ostrage, I have had my head in a hole ever since.

Writing this book at age 86 might heal part of the hurt.

The First GayPride Parade by Jeri Lee

My son called Kathy Dad

When Kathy and I started our life together, I had two sons, one of which lived with their father, and the youngest chose to live with us. He called his father his father but called Kathy his DAD. Kathy died in 1991, and his father died in 2018, but even now, in 2025, he identifies them in the same way. Kathy had no Kids.

My son went to most of the Gay shows with us and was a great addition because all the guys loved him, and he was a born salesman. He was not homosexual, but the Queens loved to pat his leather butt. At the shows that served beer, and that was most of them, he smelled like a beer can but did not drink. He would walk around the dance area and stomp beer cans because he took the aluminum home to sell. He also collected the teards from Ali that appeared in our yard and made them into teard-birds to sell at the shows. Making sure they were dry, he coated them with acrylic and used pipe cleaners for the legs. He mounted them on a small square platform to build a bird. The small teards became heads, and the larger ones became bodies. With a toothpick as a beak and feathers as wings he gave birth to his teardbitds.

Then, to make them more appealing, he gave them trophies such as a golf club, tennis racket, cups, or gadgets to hold, and called them Turd-Birds. Today, at age 62, he never married, never turned gay, and has no kids but takes excellent care of this old lady.

Son on Ali, the horse that lead the First Gay Palade in L.A. on June 28. 1970.

My Friends and the Giants of CSW

Moris Kight

Morris Kight emerged as a pivotal figure in the LGBTQ+ rights movement in Los Angeles during the mid-20th century. Born in 1923 in Lincoln, Nebraska, Kight's journey to becoming a prominent activist began in the context of a society that was largely intolerant of queer identities. After relocating to Los Angeles, he became deeply involved in the burgeoning gay rights movement. His activism was marked by a commitment to securing legal and social equality for LGBTQ+ individuals, making him a key player in the fight against discrimination and oppression.

Kight's influence was particularly felt in the 1970s when he co-founded the first gay pride parade in Los Angeles in 1970, an event that would set the stage for the annual celebrations we see today. This early parade was not just a celebration of identity but also a protest against the systemic injustices faced by the LGBTQ+ community. Kight understood the importance of visibility and representation, and he advocated for a gathering that would allow LGBTQ+ individuals to express pride in their identities while challenging societal norms. His efforts marked a significant turning point in the LGBTQ+ history of Los Angeles, as they helped to foster a sense of community and solidarity among diverse groups.

In addition to his work on the pride parade, Kight was instrumental in founding several organizations to advocate for LGBTQ+ rights. He played a significant role in establishing the Gay Community Services Center, which offered crucial resources and support to LGBTQ+ individuals. His activism extended into the political realm, where he worked tirelessly to influence legislation that would protect the rights of LGBTQ+ individuals.

The First GayPride Parade by Jeri Lee

Kight's dedication to activism was driven by a personal commitment to creating a world where LGBTQ+ people could live openly and authentically without fear of discrimination or violence.

Kight's relationship with Hollywood also exemplified the interplay between culture and activism. He recognized the power of media and entertainment to influence public perceptions of LGBTQ+ individuals. By engaging with artists and filmmakers, Kight helped shape narratives portraying LGBTQ+ lives and experiences in a more nuanced and positive light. His collaborations with notable figures in the entertainment industry not only amplified the visibility of the LGBTQ+ community but also challenged the stereotypes and stigmas that often permeated mainstream culture.

Morris Kight's legacy is a testament to the power of grassroots activism and community building. His contributions laid the groundwork for the vibrant LGBTQ+ culture in Los Angeles today. As we reflect on the history of LGBTQ+ parades and the ongoing struggle for equality, we must honor the trailblazers like Kight who fought tirelessly for the rights and recognition of LGBTQ+ individuals. Their efforts remind us that pride is a celebration and a continued call to action for justice, inclusion, and acceptance in society.

The First GayPride Parade by Jeri Lee

Troy Perry emerged as a pivotal figure in the history of LGBTQ+ activism in Los Angeles during the 1960s. As the founder of the Metropolitan Community Church (MCC) in 1968, Rev. Perry created a spiritual haven for LGBTQ+ individuals when mainstream churches largely rejected them. His vision was to establish a welcoming environment where people could embrace their identities without fear of condemnation. The MCC quickly became a sanctuary for many, combining a message of acceptance with progressive social ideals, which would resonate deeply in the burgeoning gay rights movementof body text

Rev Troy Perry

Rev. Perry's activism extended beyond the church walls. He was instrumental in organizing one of the first gay pride parades in Los Angeles, which took place in 1970. This event marked a significant shift in how LGBTQ+ individuals expressed their identities publicly. Rev. Perry's ability to unite various factions within the community demonstrated the power of collective action. The parade celebrated identity and resilience, showcasing the vibrant diversity of the LGBTQ+ population in Los Angeles. It was a bold statement against the prevailing societal norms that marginalized gay individuals.

The influence of Hollywood during this period cannot be overstated. As a city known for its entertainment industry, Los Angeles became a cultural beacon for gay rights activism, with figures like Rev. Troy Perry leading the charge. Rev. Perry's efforts attracted the attention of various artists and celebrities, which helped amplify the visibility of the LGBTQ+ movement. This intersection of activism and celebrity culture played a crucial role in normalizing LGBTQ+ identities in the public consciousness, paving the way for future generations of activists.

Rev. Perry's legacy is also marked by his commitment to advocacy beyond the religious sphere. He spoke out against discrimination and violence faced by the LGBTQ+ community, advocating for equal rights and protections. His efforts played a significant role in the early formation of coalitions that would later unite various LGBTQ+ organizations across the country. Rev. Troy Perry fought for the rights of individuals and sought to change the societal perceptions surrounding LGBTQ+ identities, making strides toward a more inclusive society.

Today, Rev. Troy Perry is celebrated as a religious leader and a pioneer in the fight for LGBTQ+ rights. His contributions to early activism in Los Angeles laid the groundwork for the vibrant pride celebrations that continue to thrive in the city. As we reflect on the history of LGBTQ+ parades and the evolution of pride, we must recognize the tireless efforts of individuals like Rev. Perry, whose vision and determination have had a lasting impact on the community. His story serves as a reminder of the power of activism and the importance of creating spaces where everyone can find acceptance and love.

ts

The First GayPride Parade by Jeri Lee

.

Rev. Bob Humphries played a significant role in the early LGBTQ+ activism landscape of Los Angeles, emerging as a pivotal figure during a time when openly gay was fraught with challenges. As a founding member of several organizations aimed at advocating for LGBTQ+ rights, Humphries dedicated his efforts to not only raising awareness but also promoting acceptance within broader society. His activism coincided with a period of heightened visibility for LGBTQ+ individuals, setting the stage for what would become a vibrant community in Los Angeles.

Rev. Humphries' contributions were not limited to advocacy; he also played a crucial role in organizing some of the earliest pride events in Los Angeles. These gatherings, which initially began as small protests, grew into more significant celebrations of identity and community. Rev. Bob understood the importance of visibility and representation, believing that public demonstrations could challenge societal norms and foster a sense of belonging among LGBTQ+ individuals. His tireless work helped lay the groundwork for what would into the grand parades that Los Angeles is known for today. eventually evolve

Bob Humphries

The First GayPride Parade by Jeri Lee

In addition to his grassroots organizing, Humphries utilized his connections within Hollywood to amplify the message of LGBTQ+ rights. Recognizing the power of media and entertainment in shaping public perception, he collaborated with artists and filmmakers to create content that highlighted the experiences and struggles of the gay community. This intersection of activism and Hollywood not only influenced how LGBTQ+ individuals were portrayed in film and television but also encouraged more members of the community to embrace their identities openly.

Rev. Humphries faced numerous obstacles throughout his activism, yet his resilience inspired many. He often spoke about the necessity of unity within the LGBTQ+ community, emphasizing that collective action was essential for effecting real change. His leadership style encouraged collaboration among various community factions, fostering an inclusive atmosphere that welcomed diverse voices and perspectives. This emphasis on solidarity helped strengthen ties between LGBTQ+ activists and their allies, creating a broader coalition for social justice.

The legacy of Rev. Bob Humphries is evident in the vibrant LGBTQ+ pride celebrations that thrive in Los Angeles today. His commitment to activism and community-building laid the foundation for future generations to advocate for their rights and celebrate their identities without fear. As LGBTQ+ pride parades became more mainstream, they also retained the spirit of resistance that figures like Humphries instilled, reminding us that the fight for equality is ongoing. His story serves as a testament to the power of individual action in shaping history and inspiring hope within the LGBTQ+ community.

The First GayPride Parade by Jeri Lee

IPat Rocco was a significant figure in the early LGBTQ+ movement in Los Angeles, known for his pioneering work as a filmmaker and activist. Born in 1931, Rocco became a prominent voice during a time when LGBTQ+ individuals faced rampant discrimination and societal ostracism. His contributions to gay cinema challenged the existing stereotypes and provided a platform for expressing gay identity in a way that was both accessible and relatable to a broader audience. Rocco's films were often characterized by their bold portrayal of gay

Pat Rocco.

relationships, showcasing love and intimacy that was rarely seen in mainstream media.

In the 1960s and 1970s, Rocco's work emerged during a transformative period for LGBTQ+ rights, coinciding with the burgeoning gay liberation movement. He utilized his talent to create films that entertained and educated viewers about the struggles and joys of being gay. Rocco's films often featured strong narratives that highlighted the complexities of gay life, breaking away from the conventional narratives that often marginalized LGBTQ+ experiences. His ability to depict genuine emotional connections between characters provided desperately needed representation at the time.

Rocco's impact extended beyond the realm of filmmaking. He was an early participant in the gay pride movement, utilizing his art to advocate for LGBTQ+ visibility and rights. His participation in early pride events in Los Angeles helped shape the culture surrounding these

The First GayPride Parade by Jeri Lee

gatherings, fostering community and solidarity among participants. By actively engaging in pride parades and other LGBTQ+ events, Rocco not only celebrated gay identity but also encouraged others to embrace their own identities without fear of judgment or persecution. The influence of Hollywood on gay culture cannot be overstated, and Rocco's work exemplified the intersection of art and activism in Los Angeles. He was part of a generation of artists who sought to redefine the narrative surrounding homosexuality in media. Through his films and public appearances, Rocco became a symbol of resistance against the oppressive norms of the time. His legacy is a reminder of how creativity can be a powerful tool for social change, inspiring future generations to continue the fight for equality and representation. Rocco's contributions to LGBTQ+ culture in Los Angeles continue to resonate today. His films are celebrated for their artistic merit and their role in paving the way for future LGBTQ+ filmmakers and activists. As pride celebrations evolved into vibrant expressions of identity and community, Rocco's early work laid the groundwork for the cultural landscape we see today. His story is an essential chapter in the history of LGBTQ+ activism, reminding us of the courage and creativity propelling the movement forward.

Gay Symbols form the lambda to the Rainbow Flag

The eleventh lower-case letter of the Greek alphabet, the forerunner of the letter L, was initially pictured as the scales of balance; the Greeks believed balance was a reconciliation between two opposites: an unstable state needing constant adjusting. They added a hook to the base of the letter to indicate some action was necessary. Spartans adopted the lambda as a symbol of their unity, believing that the demands of society should never interfere with a person's right to be totally free and independent, and only in a common bond could they hope to preserve their existence as free and equal people. The Romans saw the shape as suggestive of a flame and used it as a symbol for their Latin word, torch.

Scientists seeking a symbol for the wavelength of light used lamba because of its historical past and connection with the torch. As a symbol of freedom for the Gay and Lesbian community, the lambda represents the light of knowledge shed into the darkness of ignorance, a promise of hope, and a new future with dignity. Thus the lambda, with all its meaning, is an especially apt symbol for the gay liberation movement, which energetically seeks a balance in society and which strives through enlightenment to secure equal rights for homosexual people. It is the international symbol for gay rights.

We went from Lamda to the rainbow flag as the leading Gay symbol. Choosing a rainbow is making a silent statement that homosexuality is as normal and natural and beautiful as a rainbow. Over the years, it has had many names, such as the Rainbow flag, the Gay flag, the Gay Pride flag, and now mostly just the Pride Flag. This tradition started in San Francisco, California, and is now worldwide.

The LGBTQ community wears and uses the rainbow in many items as freely and with the same meaning as the flag. So it is not the flag that is the outward symbol of their identity or support it is the rainbow. In the 60's, I was a hippie, I burnt my bra, and we claimed the rainbow flag before the LGBTQ community resurrected it.

The Rainbow Flag

The Gay Rainbow flag has given a colorful aura to all LGBTQ functions.
It was well accepted by the global LGBTQ community but resented by the straight world, which thinks it is part of Mother Nature and that she is straight.
It regrettably does not obey the prism for the word Rainbow, but it reflects an impressive image. The colors keep changing along with their meanings, but as a flag, it represents hope, unity, and love regardless of gender, ethnicity, or labels.

Harvey Milk, the first openly gay elected official in the history of California, commissioned Gilbert Baker to create an image of pride for the gay community. He designed this 8-stripe flag to represent the diversity of the LGBTQ+ community. Recognizing that flags are one of the most essential characteristics of self-identity, the design was printed onto a flag and presented to the LGBTQ community during the Gay Freedom Day parade of 1978 in San Francisco.

It was inspired by the lyrics of Judy Garland's Over the Rainbow. Even though the original was widely accepted over the years, every group claiming allegiance wanted to change something about it to custom-make it just for their group.

It has become an iconic representation of freedom, equality, and unity, and most observers don't realize that strip colors matter. They instantly relate to the rainbow flag, which can be any rainbow flag as being a Gay flag.

Baker hand-dyed, and hand-sewed the flag, which flew at the San Francisco Gay Freedom Day in June 1978.

The First GayPride Parade by Jeri Lee

Add a little bit The evolution of Pride events is inherently tied to the history and symbolism of the rainbow flag, which emerged as a beacon of hope and a unifying emblem for the LGBTQ community. The flag consisted of eight colors, each representing different aspects of the human experience: life, healing, sunlight, nature, harmony, spirit, and more. Over time, this vibrant community rallied around this emblem, Pride events began flourishing as celebrations of identity and demonstrations for equality.

The first Pride parade in Los Angeles, CA, in 1970 marked a pivotal moment in LGBTQ history, commemorating the first anniversary of the Stonewall riots. Initially, these events were small and often met with hostility, reflecting the societal stigma surrounding homosexuality. However, as the community grew more organized and vocal, Pride events expanded in size and scope. Cities across the globe started to adopt the rainbow flag, transforming it into a symbol of resistance and resilience, ultimately giving rise to the diverse Pride celebrations we see today.

As Pride events evolved, they became platforms for celebrating identity and advocating for rights and social change. The rainbow flag, with its rich symbolism, served as a rallying point for various movements, from the fight against HIV/AIDS in the 1980s to contemporary efforts for transgender rights and racial justice within the LGBTQ community. Participants of the first Gay Parade often recount the energy and determination that permeated those early gatherings, setting the stage for future events embracing intersectionality and inclusivity.

The First GayPride Parade by Jeri Lee

The growth of Pride events also reflects broader societal changes in attitudes towards the LGBTQ community. As acceptance increased, so did the visibility of Pride celebrations, which began to attract allies and supporters from all walks of life. Once a symbol of defiance, the rainbow flag became a representation of love and solidarity, inspiring a global movement that transcended borders. This transformation is evident in the diverse ways Pride events are celebrated today, with parades, festivals, and educational initiatives that promote awareness and understanding.

The evolution of Pride events is a testament to the power of community and the enduring impact of the rainbow flag. From its humble beginnings in the aftermath of the Stonewall riots to today's vibrant, multifaceted celebrations, Pride has become a vital expression of identity and activism. As participants of the first Gay Parade share their personal stories, they illuminate the journey of an entire community, showcasing how the simple act of coming together under a flag can foster change and inspire future generations to embrace their true selves.

PinkTriangle

Another significant symbol was the pink triangle, which originated during the Holocaust as a marker for gay men in concentration camps. In the 1970s, the pink triangle was reclaimed as a symbol of pride and resistance against oppression. Participants wore this emblem to honor the historical suffering of LGBTQ individuals and to recognize the ongoing fight against discrimination and violence. The act of wearing the pink triangle transformed a symbol of shame into one of empowerment and defiance, illustrating the community's resilience in the face of adversity

The iconic symbols and their meanings from Gay history and enforced by the first Gay Parade in Los Angeles serve as a historical lens through which we can examine the evolution of LGBTQ rights and identity. They not only represent the struggles and triumphs of the past but also continue to inspire future generations. As we reflect on these symbols, we acknowledge the courage of those who marched in 1970,

paving the way for the vibrant, diverse, and inclusive celebrations that are a hallmark of Pride events today. Understanding the significance of these symbols allows the community to honor its history while fostering a collective identity that transcends time and space.

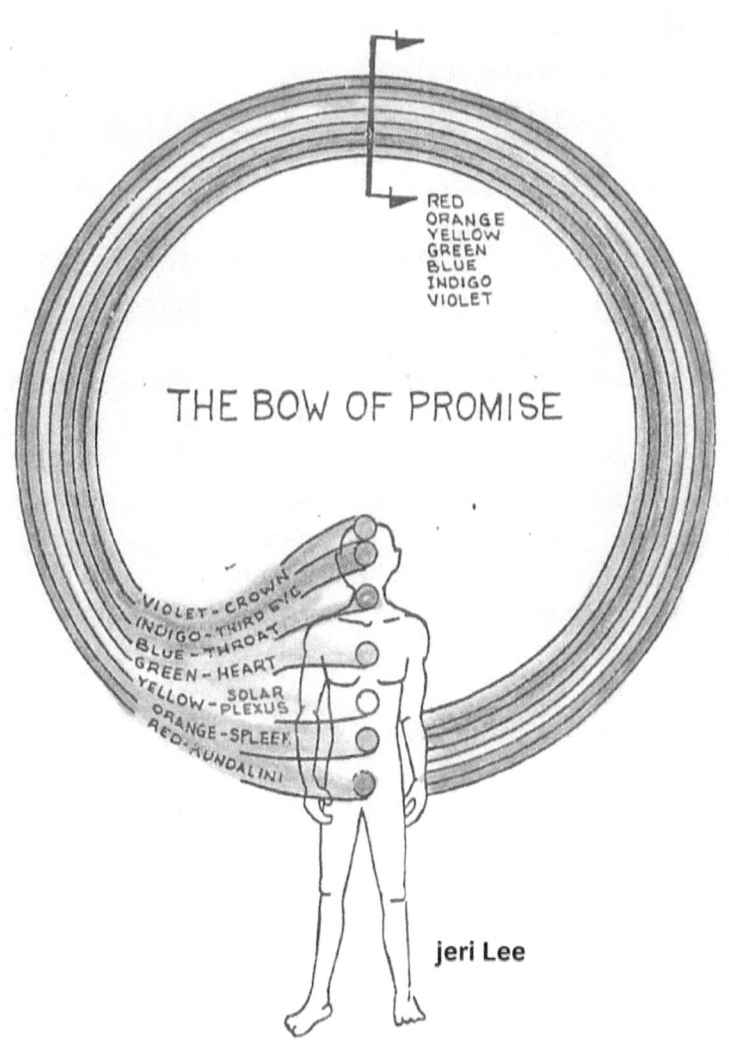

RED
ORANGE
YELLOW
GREEN
BLUE
INDIGO
VIOLET

THE BOW OF PROMISE

VIOLET - CROWN
INDIGO - THIRD EYE
BLUE - THROAT
GREEN - HEART
YELLOW - SOLAR PLEXUS
ORANGE - SPLEEN
RED - KUNDALINI

jeri Lee

You are a
RAINBOW
Your CHAKRAS

The First GayPride Parade by Jeri Lee

Contact: White House Press Office, 202-456-2100
WASHINGTON, June 2
The following was released today by the White House:
GAY AND LESBIAN PRIDE MONTH, 2000
BY THE PRESIDENT OF THE UNITED STATES OF AMERICA,
A PROCLAMATION:

Gay and lesbian Americans have made important and lasting contributions to our Nation in every field of endeavor. Too often, however, gays and lesbians face prejudice and discrimination; too many have had to hide or deny their sexual orientation in order to keep their jobs or to live safely in their communities.

In recent years, we have made some progress righting these wrongs. Since the Stonewall uprising in New York City more than 30 years ago, the gay and lesbian rights movement has united gays and lesbians, their families and friends, and all those committed to justice and equality in a crusade to outlaw discriminatory laws and practices and to protect gays and lesbians from prejudice and persecution.

I am proud of the part that my Administration has played to achieve these goals. Today, more openly gay and lesbian individuals serve in senior posts throughout the Federal Government than during any other Administration.

To build on our progress, in 1998 I issued an Executive Order to prohibit discrimination in the Federal civilian workforce based on sexual orientation, and my Administration continues to fight for the Employment Non-Discrimination Act, which would outlaw discrimination in the workplace based on sexual orientation.

Yet many challenges still lie before us. As we have learned from recent tragedies, prejudice against gays and lesbians can still erupt into acts of hatred and violence. I continue to call upon the Congress to pass meaningful hate crimes legislation to strengthen the Department of Justice's ability to prosecute hate crimes committed due to the victim's sexual orientation. With each passing year the American people become more receptive to diversity and more open to those who are different from themselves. Our Nation is at last realizing that gays and lesbians must no longer bed

The First GayPride Parade by Jeri Lee

"strangers among friends," as the civil rights pioneer David Mixner once noted. Rather, we must finally recognize these Americans for what they are: our colleagues and neighbors, daughters and sons, sisters and brothers, friends and partners.

This June, recognizing the joys and sorrows that the gay and lesbian movement has witnessed and the work that remains to be done, we observe Gay and Lesbian Pride Month and celebrate the progress we have made in creating a society more inclusive and accepting of gays and lesbians. I hope that in this new millennium we will continue to break down the walls of fear and prejudice and work to build a bridge to understanding and tolerance, until gays and lesbians are afforded the same rights and responsibilities as all Americans.

NOW, THEREFORE, I, WILLIAM J. CLINTON, President of the United States of America, by virtue of the authority vested in me by the Constitution and laws of the United States, do hereby proclaim June 2000 as G ay and Lesbian Pride Month. I encourage all Americans to observe this month with appropriate programs, ceremonies, and activities that celebrate our diversity and recognize the gay and lesbian Americans whose many and varied contributions have enriched our national life.

IN WITNESS WHEREOF, I have hereunto set my hand this second day of June, in the year of our Lord two thousand, and of the Independence of the United States of America the two hundred and twenty-fourth.

WILLIAM J. CLINTON

the First Gay Parade

the Birth of Global Pride

The First GayPride Parade by Jeri Lee

Pride  **Month**

The first pride marches were held in four US cities on June 28, 1970, one year after the riots at the Stonewall Inn. The New York City march was promoted as "Christopher Street Liberation Day," alongside parallel marches in Chicago, Los Angeles, and San Francisco. Los Angeles was the only one with a parade permit, classifying it as the First gay parade. June became recognized as Pride Month in the United States to commemorate the Stonewall Uprising. President Bill Clinton officially declared in a presidential proclamation in June "Gay and Lesbian Pride Month" in 1999. Barack Obama expanded the official Pride Month recognition in 2011, including the whole of the LGBT community; Donald Trump declined to offer federal recognition of Pride Month in 2017, though he issued supportive public statements in a series of Tweets in 2019. Joe Biden recognized Pride Month after taking office in 2021 and vowed to push for LGBT rights in the United States, despite previously voting against same-sex marriages and school education on LGBT topics in the Senate. Pride Month has since become a global celebration of LGBTQ+ culture and identity.

We have come
A
LONG WAY

JUNE IS
PRIDE
MONTH

The First GayPride Parade by Jeri Lee

The Social Climate of the 1960s

The 1960s marked a pivotal decade in the evolution of social attitudes toward race, gender, and sexuality, setting the stage for significant changes that would culminate in the first Gay Parade in Los Angeles in 1970. This period was characterized by widespread social upheaval as marginalized groups began to assert their rights and identities more vocally.

The civil rights movement, anti-war protests, and the counterculture revolution collectively influenced the LGBTQ+ community, creating an environment ripe for activism and a reexamination of societal norms. As individuals began to reject the constraints of traditional gender roles and sexual orientation, the seeds of the modern gay rights movement were sown, and I was in the middle of it.

In the 1960s, homosexuality was primarily criminalized and stigmatized, with most LGB individuals living in fear of persecution. However, the decade also saw the emergence of organizations such as the Mattachine Society and the Daughters of Bilitis, which provided safe spaces for gay and lesbian individuals to meet and discuss their experiences.

These organizations advocated for the decriminalization of homosexuality and fought against discrimination, laying the groundwork for the activism that would gain momentum in the following years. The Stonewall Riots of 1969 was a crucial turning point, galvanizing LGB individuals and allies to unite in their fight for visibility and rights, ultimately inspiring the creation of pride events across the country.

The First GayPride Parade by Jeri Lee

The cultural landscape of the 1960s significantly influenced the expression of identity within the LGBTQ+ community. The era's fashion and art movements, which emphasized self-expression and individuality, resonated with many gay individuals seeking to assert their identities. The visibility of LGBTQ+ figures in popular culture and the growing acceptance of alternative lifestyles encouraged many to embrace their identities openly. Symbols of pride and resistance began to emerge, foreshadowing the vibrant expressions of identity that would characterize the first Gay Parade in Los Angeles.

Media coverage of LGBTQ+ issues during the 1960s was often sensationalized or negative, yet it also provided a platform for activists to share their narratives. Publications such as The Advocate began to circulate, offering a voice to the community and highlighting the struggles and triumphs of LGBTQ+ individuals.

As the decade progressed, more mainstream media outlets started to cover stories related to the gay rights movement, albeit often through a lens of misunderstanding. This complex relationship with the media would shape public perceptions and reactions to the first Gay Parade and future pride events.

The social climate of the 1960s created a fertile ground for the emergence of pride events as a form of activism.

The convergence of various social movements, combined with a growing sense of solidarity among LGBTQ+ individuals, led to the realization that visibility was essential for change. The first Gay Parade in Los Angeles in 1970 was not just a celebration but a declaration of existence and a demand for equality. It represented the culmination of years of struggle and the beginning of a new era in LGBTQ+ activism that would continue to evolve and inspire future generations.

The First GavPride Parade bv Jeri Lee

Preceding Events Leading to the Parade

The events leading up to the first gay parade in Los Angeles on June 28, 1970, were shaped by a confluence of social, political, and personal factors that galvanized the LGBTQ+ community to take a stand. The late 1960s were marked by a growing awareness of civil rights movements, including the fight for racial equality and women's iberation.

These movements inspired LGBTQ+ individuals to unite and assert their rights in a society that was increasingly hostile to their existence. The Stonewall riots in New York City in 1969 served as a critical catalyst, igniting a sense of urgency and solidarity among gay individuals nationwide. This pivotal event not only highlighted the need for visibility but also encouraged activists to organize events that would honor the struggles faced by the community.

In Los Angeles, the groundwork for the parade began to take shape as local activists recognized the need to create a platform for expression and visibility. Individuals like Morris Kight and others from the Gay Liberation Front played instrumental roles in planning the event. They sought to create a space where LGBTQ+ individuals could unite, celebrate their identities, and demand equality. The atmosphere was charged with a sense of hope and determination, as many believed this parade could begin a new era for LGBTQ+ rights. Planning meetings were held in various community spaces, bringing together a diverse group of deeply committed individuals to the cause.

As the parade date approached, the community mobilized to spread the word and gather support. Flyers were distributed, and local businesses began to support the event.

The First GayPride Parade by Jeri Lee

The media, although often hesitant to cover LGBTQ+ issues, began to take notice as the parade gained momentum. This increasing visibility helped frame the event as a celebration and a pivotal moment in the fight for civil rights. Activists emphasized the importance of participation, appealing to individuals who had previously felt marginalized or voiceless. The call for unity resonated strongly, and many felt that their personal stories and struggles could be shared on this grand stage.

The fashion and symbols of identity that emerged in the lead-up to the parade were also significant. Participants began creating banners, wearing distinctive clothing, and adopting symbols representing their pride and resistance. The preparation for the parade became an act of empowerment, as individuals expressed their identities in bold and creative ways.

On the eve of the parade, excitement mingled with anxiety as participants reflected on the historical significance of what they were about to undertake. For many, this was not just a parade but a declaration of existence in a world that had long sought to silence them.

The atmosphere was electric, filled with anticipation and a sense of purpose. The collective resolve to challenge societal norms and advocate for change set the stage for what would become a landmark event in LGBTQ+ history. The first gay parade in Los Angeles was a celebration of identity and a bold statement of defiance against oppression, laying the foundation for future activism and pride events.

The First GayPride Parade by Jeri Lee

Stonewall Riots

The Stonewall Riots, which erupted in June 1969 in New York City, served as a significant catalyst for the modern LGBTQ+ rights movement. This pivotal event marked a turning point in the fight for equality and justice, inspiring countless individuals across the United States, including those in Los Angeles. The confrontations between patrons of the Stonewall Inn and law enforcement revealed the deep-seated frustrations within the gay community regarding police harassment and societal discrimination.

This unrest ignited a sense of urgency and solidarity, prompting activists to organize and mobilize in ways previously unseen.
In the aftermath of Stonewall, the call for pride and visibility resonated deeply within the LGBTQ+ community, which at that time was only LGB. The message was clear: no longer would Homosexuals hide in the shadows or accept the status quo. This newfound spirit of resistance manifested itself in planning the first Gay Parade in Los Angeles in June 1970, which was not merely a celebration but a powerful statement of identity and defiance.

Participants aimed to honor the bravery of those who fought at Stonewall while advocating for their rights and demanding societal acceptance.

The historical significance of the 1970 Gay Parade in L.A. cannot be overstated. It represented a collective affirmation of identity and a public declaration of existence, where individuals came together to challenge the stigma surrounding their lives.

The parade served as a platform for voices that had long been silenced, allowing participants to express their individuality and pride openly.

The event also garnered attention from the media, amplifying its message and spreading awareness about the truggles faced by the LGBTQ+ community.

The legacy of the Stonewall Riots and the subsequent L.A. Gay Parade continues to influence contemporary pride events. As the movement has evolved, the core principles of activism, visibility, and solidarity remain integral to the LGBTQ+ experience. The struggles faced in the 1970s laid the groundwork for ongoing advocacy and legislative changes, reminding us of the importance of remembering and honoring our past. The stories from that era serve as both a celebration of progress and a reminder of the work that still lies ahead in pursuing equality and justice for all.

The First GayPride Parade by Jeri Lee

Public Perception and Backlash

Public perception of the first gay parade in Los Angeles on June 28, 1970, was a complex mixture of curiosity, skepticism, and outright hostility. For many in the broader society, the event represented a radical departure from the norms of the time. It was a public display of identity and pride that challenged deeply ingrained societal values. Those who witnessed the parade found themselves confronting a reality that had largely been hidden from view. Participants in this historic event took to the streets with vibrant colors and bold slogans, signaling a shift in the cultural landscape and inviting both support and backlash from various segments of the community.

The reaction from the media played a significant role in shaping public perception. Coverage ranged from supportive to sensationalist, often emphasizing the more scandalous aspects of the event rather than its core message of equality and rights. While some outlets highlighted the bravery of participants, others perpetuated stereotypes that marginalized the movement. This dichotomy in media representation contributed to a polarized public response, where some embraced the parade as a sign of progress, while others viewed it as a threat to traditional values. The media's framing of the event had lasting implications, influencing how LGBTQ individuals were perceived and treated in society.

Backlash from conservative groups underscored the tensions surrounding the parade. Many organizations condemned the event, framing it as an affront to family values and societal norms. These groups mobilized to voice their discontent, organizing counter-protests and disseminating pamphlets that sought to discredit the LGBTQ+ community. The backlash was not only vocal but also manifest in legislative efforts aimed at stifling the growing movement for LGBTQ+ rights. This resistance highlighted the challenges faced

The First GayPride Parade by Jeri Lee

by activists who were determined to push for visibility and acceptance in a society that still largely rejected their existence.

Amidst the backlash, the strength and resilience of the LGBTQ+ community shone through. Participants viewed the parade as an opportunity to reclaim their narratives and assert their identities. Personal stories from those who marched reveal a profound sense of empowerment and solidarity that emerged from the event. For many, the parade was a declaration of self-acceptance and a call for recognition. This spirit of defiance in the face of adversity fostered a sense of unity within the community, encouraging further activism and engagement in the fight for rights.

The first gay parade in Los Angeles ultimately served as a catalyst for change, igniting a broader conversation about LGBTQ rights and paving the way for future pride events. While public perception was fraught with tension and division, the parade marked a pivotal moment in history, inspiring generations to come. The stories of those who participated not only reflect the struggles of the time but also highlight the importance of visibility, activism, and the ongoing quest for equality. As the LGBTQ community continues to evolve, understanding the complexities of public perception and backlash during this formative period remains crucial in appreciating the significance of pride and the fight for rights today.

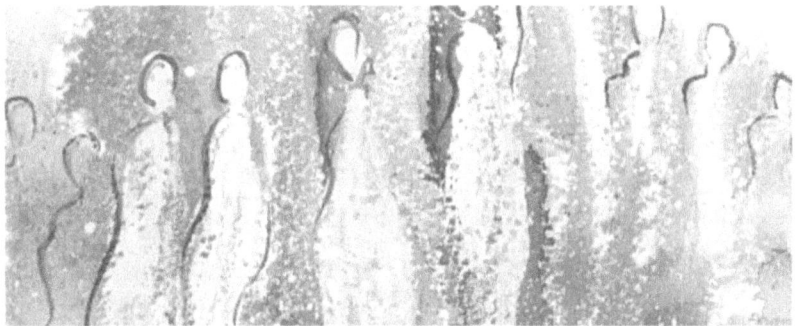

The First GayPride Parade by Jeri Lee

Confronting Opposition
Christian turn or burners

The first gay parade held in a major city was more than just a celebration; it was a poignant reminder of the struggles faced by the LGBTQ community. For many participants, the event culminated in years spent grappling with their identities, societal rejection, and fear.

Confronting opposition during the early days of the gay rights movement was both a personal and collective struggle. Participants of the first gay parade faced resistance not only from societal norms but also from their own internalized fears and doubts. The need for visibility and acceptance clashed with the deeply rooted prejudices of the time, creating a complex landscape where courage was essential. Many individuals recount their experiences navigating this opposition, revealing how it shaped their identities and fortitude as activists. The act of stepping into the spotlight, despite the shadows of disapproval, became a defining moment for many.

The opposition participants faced was multifaceted, ranging from familial rejection to hostility from law enforcement and the general public. Many individuals who joined the parade had to grapple with the fear of losing loved ones or even their jobs and facing violence simply for expressing their true selves. These fears were not unfounded; reports of harassmen

The First GayPride Parade by Jeri Lee

Shaping Future Generations

Shaping future generations involves more than just celebrating past achievements; it requires a commitment to education, visibility, and advocacy that can influence the minds and hearts of those who come after us. The first gay parade was not just a moment of joy but a pivotal event that would inspire countless individuals to embrace their identities and advocate for their rights. By sharing personal stories from participants, we can shed light on the struggles and triumphs that paved the way for the acceptance and rights enjoyed today. These narratives are crucial in educating younger generations about the importance of pride, resilience, and community.

Personal stories from participants of the first gay parade reveal the diverse backgrounds and experiences that converged in a shared quest for acceptance. Many individuals faced severe repercussions for their identities before the parade, including ostracism from family and friends, discrimination in the workplace, and even violence. Through their testimonies, we learn how the parade became a turning point, transforming fear into courage and isolation into solidarity. These stories demonstrate the power of visibility and its profound impact on those who feel marginalized, showing future generations that they are not alone in their struggles.

The significance of the first gay parade extends beyond individual experiences and serves as a blueprint for activism and advocacy. The stories from participants highlight the importance of standing together and using collective voices to demand change. As we reflect on these

The First GayPride Parade by Jeri Lee

narratives, we can identify key strategies for future activists, such as the need for community organization, the importance of intersectionality, and the value of creating safe spaces. These lessons are essential for shaping future generations who will carry the torch of advocacy, reminding them that their voices matter and can enact change.

In addition to advocacy, shaping future generations also involves fostering a sense of belonging and pride within the LGBTQ community. The personal stories shared by participants reveal how the first gay parade provided a platform for self-expression and celebration of identity. These narratives illustrate the importance of community and the emotional support it offers by recounting moments of joy, laughter, and connection. Encouraging future generations to embrace their authentic selves and find their place within the community is crucial for ensuring that the progress made is recognized and sustained.

As we continue to share and amplify these personal stories, we are not just preserving history; we are actively shaping the future. By educating younger generations about the struggles and victories of those who came before them, we instill a sense of responsibility to uphold and advance the rights and visibility of the LGBTQ community. The legacy of the first gay parade is one of hope, resilience, and empowerment. We must pass that torch to future generations, ensuring they understand the importance of standing proud in the spotlight. The experiences we endured can not have a complete meaning without living them. So, my greatest wish is that the efforts and actions of my generation be appreciated and not forgotten.

Comming out before 1970

To clarify things, I was there from the beginning of this book; I did it and don't just talk about it. I moved from Conn to southern California in 1969, and that's where this book begins.

I'm not planning to expose my diary as the plot or documentary, but I will tell you that the lesbian on horseback in the first gay parade was my loving wife and that the horse was one of our cherished possessions. Also, the organizers and producers of the first Gay Parade were on my list of friends and memories. So when I speak of them, it is with some authority because I remember. I was there at a young age, but I remember well. I also remember that two of the four heroes for the success of June 28, 1970, had Rev. as a label. Rev. Troy Perry and Rev. Bob Humphries, so God must have been on our side.

At the time I came out, it was well-circulated, and my mother disowned me. She blamed herself, asking why God had punished her with such a wicked child, and ran to the bathroom crying every time somebody mentioned my name. My parents were very religious, belonging to the Baptist church where my father was a deacon. To ease her guilt and make him share his part of my Sin, she ordered him to write me a 'letter from God.' He took the biblical thesaurus, researched the word homosexual in all its forms, and copied all the biblical verses that he thought came close to matching my indictment. He hand-wrote it double-sided on 15 sheets of paper, stuffed it in a large envelope, and mailed it to me. My punishment was that my mother publicly disowned me. For some unknown reason, my father

Comming out before 1970

was not as harsh as my mother and never admitted that he shared her verdict.

Upon receipt of the said indictment, my wife Kathy Lee and I boarded Delta from L.A. to Boston with a motion to dismiss the verdict. I knew my mother could not disown me to my face. I was born number two of six siblings. There was one female, four real boys, and me. My mother's God given ranking system was that God blesses boys in order of birth and girls were their servants, but she could not label me, so she just threw me out.

Number three son met us at the airport and explained that our trip was in vain because our mother would not let me into her house. I responded, let's go home, she couldn't say no.

About four miles from the destination, we stopped for a snack to address our progress, but Mother still said no, so I instructed my brother to take me home anyway. Father opened the door while mother hid in the bathroom. I know she could not stay in there long. She finally came out with the statement, "I will not accept it, but for now, I will tolerate it."

On the return to the airport, I asked my brother, how do you feel since you have been exposed to this new fact? He replied, "When you fall into ice water, it's pretty shocking, but it's not that bad after you get used to it."

Cross Dressing was the Way to Hide

When I was young, the family, community, society, and legal world punished you for being homosexual. It was so drastic that to hide your true self, the common practice was to cross dress. That means the most feminine of the pair would dress and act female, and the other would be male.

At age 19, I was living in Htfd Conn, working at The Hartford Courant in the day while attending Hartford Art at night and on weekends working as a film stripper and Artist at a printing co.

The printing company was small, and I often worked late at night. Two men owned it; one ran the printers while the other ran the streets as the salesman.

The Salesman came in one night all excited about a new bar he had just been in, and it was something he thought his friend should witness. These men were both straight and both married. Not wanting to leave me alone at night in the printing shop, they decided to take a minor to the bar.

Well protected with a gentleman on each arm, we visited the Pink Pussycat. The Bar had two rooms. The first was smokey with the active bar, and the other had booths down one side with about six small tables with chairs and a small dance floor. There was a colorful jukebox playing on the back wall between two doors. One door marked Men the other Women.

From casual observation, the patrons appeared to be heterosexual college kids from the surrounding universities.

Having a corner booth, we had a viewing area of those two doors and watched what appeared to be men go into the women's room and women go to the men's.

My bosses were gamblers and bet on ponies, races, and sports games. So why not bet on which door the next in line would take?

So I spent the evening witnessing these two men drink Beer and gambling on who was the crossdresser. That was day one of the formal education for my future.

the Cornerstones

In sharing my experiences, I hope to contribute to the oral histories documenting the lives of prominent LGBTQ figures in Los Angeles. Each story adds depth to our understanding of the rich legacy we inherit. By recounting my own journey, I aim to inspire future generations to continue the fight for justice and equality. This chapter is not just a personal reflection; it is a testament to the strength of our community and the pride that propels us forward. It is a memory of what we had to do to survive our situation before we heard terms like gay liberation and gay rights; the story of Los Angeles CSW is one of hope, resilience, and the unwavering belief that love and acceptance will ultimately prevail.

We laid the cornerstones for today's LGBTQ rights through pivotal moments in Los Angeles's history that exploded the groundwork for national movements. In the mid-20th century, L.A. became a melting pot for LGBTQ individuals, fostering a sense of community that was both vibrant and resilient.

The city was home to early activists who fought against oppressive laws and societal norms. Their efforts addressed local issues and inspired broader movements across the United States. By analyzing these foundational moments, we can better understand and thank my friends Morris Kight, Troy Perry, Bob Humphries, and Pat Rocco for setting the groundwork for the rights and recognition the LGBTQ community enjoys today.

Homosexuality

Is as Natural as this

Rainbow

Time makes Changes, and HeartAche

I stood in front of the hearth, leaning heavily on my cane and staring into the mirror that framed the wall before me. I was looking at the reflection of an old lady, an old lady with a big story to tell. A 6-inch crystal ball cradled in its walnut holder shared the reflection; next

to it was a well-used deck of Tarot cards and three tall white candles. The ball was cold, the cards were lifeless, and the candles screamed to be lit.

To tell my story in a fashion that would be honorable to the memory of the three candles, I have to, in part, play Alice in Wonderland and fall through the mirror, but first, I have to introduce you to the angels who stand behind the candles, for they are the three major players in this true drama.

The candles are white for purity, although I can honestly say none was pure. They all had problems that life dealt to them, and they all made choices that drastically altered my life. The thread that bonds them now is that they are all dead. I am the living one, left to tell the story.

The TV blasted in the background, and the dogs barked at the cold vapors in their world, but no one else seemed to see. Tears streamed down my face as I looked past my reflection, past the tired old lady, to the TV and watched in

The First GayPride Parade by Jeri Lee

the mirror the story of Friday the 13th in February of 2004 in San Francisco, California. The mayor of the city had declared that same-sex unions could legally be declared marriages, with all the rights the law gives to marriages between man and woman. As the line of happy couples circled the block at City Hall, my heart cried because I knew if Kathy were still alive, we would fly to San Francisco to be part of this day in history.

I picked up the first candle and, with a pointed tool, engraved her name, KATHY LEE, on the face of the candle. Choking on my emotions, I lit the flame. I said to her: "Kathy, lady of my life, love of my heart, soul mate of my other side: I know that you are looking down on this day of Glory and singing cheers and praises, knowing that you played a part in laying the foundation of Gay Liberation, knowing that you were a pebble in the cornerstone of all the happy unions taking place at this time.

I remember when I lived in Anaheim, California... with my husband and two small sons, and the TV was blasting another story of a gay marriage. This time, it was two lesbians dressed in Levis and faded blue denim work shirts who stood on a bench in the center of a well-known park in

The First GayPride Parade by Jeri Lee

an exclusive suburb of Los Angeles and declared their love for each other in a public wedding ceremony. Helen Niehaus, the president of a local private gay club called "The Society Anubis," did the honors. I later found out that the names of those two lesbians were Kathy Lee and Kathy Fina, and I would soon make it a trio.

I salute you, Kathy Lee, for also being a part of the First Gay Parade in Los Angeles on June 28, 1970 As you and your horse Ali led the first L.A. Gay Parade down Hollywood Blvd.

To you, Kathy Lee, I renew my respect and love because I know that if Death had not crept into our lives like a thief in the night and stolen you from me, that we would be proudly standing in that line in the streets of San Francisco, patiently waiting for our turn to declare to the world that all persons have a right to be declared "united in matrimony."

The flame flickered as I held her candle high and offered my blessings to the life of a great person. My heartfelt young with pride, but my reflection glared back at me, telling another story. It has been many years that I have mourned and felt sorry for myself for my loss, many years that I had tried to stay alive despite many health issues, many years of battling the demons that surrounded your Death, and many years of facing my fears. Yes, Kathy Lee, when you took your last breath, I held your right hand, and Kathy Fina held your left. We kissed your forehead, blessed your spirit, and left the hospital room together.

the First Gay Pride Parade   Jeri Lee

I placed the candle on its holder, picked up the next one, and engraved in its surface the name of Kathy Fina with my tool. I lit the candle and remembered that horrible day when I received the call that Kathy Fina was found hanging in a motel room in Riverside, California, a victim of her own doing. The image was etched in my imagination and sealed with "what if..." and "what if I had..." and "could I have done something to stop her from taking her own life?" She knew the pain of being a lesbian and understood the meaning of "stand up and die," but why this way? My heart smiles with only one glimmer of light, knowing my two Kathys are together.

Ruth Zachary

the First Gay Pride Parade   Jeri Lee

Now, I engraved the price tag of one cent for the last candle, lighting it and placing it in line. One cent for Penny, born Pansy Fae Carter, and remembered the price I paid for my first lesbian relationship. I swallowed hard, trying to forget that night the phone rang and awakened me at 3 a.m., and from the far end of the line, the bewildered voice that sounded drunk, blabbering about something like her landlord and her dog was lost, and many things that made no sense. Was I wrong to tell her, "Penny, call me tomorrow when you are sober and can talk straight?" I will never know, for her daughter called me four days later saying they had just found her mother dead of an overdose of pills and that she had been dead for several days. After checking the phone bill, they estimated that I was the last person she talked to before killing herself.

I shut my eyes and took three deep breaths to compose myself, then slowly opened them. Chills ran up my spine, and the hair on my arms stood tall. I was engulfed in an icy cold while three columns of mist were standing behind me.

The road to gay liberation has been paved with a history of issues. Today's big question on gay marriage is not just an issue; it is our right. Many persons, big and small, have stood up to be counted, and I salute them all. I am only one small voice, but I was there along with millions of others, and collectively, we are strong and will see Victory.

the First Gay Pride Parade   Jeri Lee

THE HAND THAT WRITES UPON THE WALL

We use to share all the joys of life,
And I proudly called you my wife.
Death was the thief that stole you from me.
Now, you're the hand that writes upon the wall.

You used to sing all your love songs to me.
You used to smile and call me, "Your thee."
Now you sing with the heavenly host,
And you're the hand that writes upon the wall.

We used to talk of future things,
That we would do when we were old.
Now you watch over me from above
and are the hand that writes upon the wall.

Earthly wealth we proudly gained,
For dollar values, we were insane.
I would trade it all for a one-night stand.
With the hand that writes upon my wall.

I know one day we'll meet again,
We'll laugh and cry as we did then.
We'll live and love and never part, for:
You're the hand that wrote upon my heart.

LESBIAN

Jeri Lee

Poems by Jeri Lee

Reflections

Ruth Zachary

Hello mirror on the wall
I have no secrets you tell all.
Behind this wrinkled face of age
A child of memory plays on my stage.
The riddle of time has etched life's change
While deep inside I remain the same.
For others I wear the mask of fate
I took time to live is how I rate.
The ups and downs the good and bad
Life's challenges were often sad.
Though the body grows old the mind stays
young
The spirit is actively searching for fun.
So old lady just step aside
And let my memories take a ride.

Prisoner of Time
Cuffed by life and sentenced to death
Destiny in every breath
The direction of choice is totally mine
Good or bad, I am a prisoner of time
The gridlines you walk are not by chance
For we are part of a cosmic dance.
The rhythms of nature, the riddle of time
This global footprint is totally mine
Dharma in and karma out
This incarnation is a turnabout
You face your past day after day
Good deeds to others are how you pay
You end up at the end of the road
Thinking you've cracked the cosmic code
You stand in line for your just-due
To find your reward was ---
Finding You.
by Jeri Lee

WHERE AM I
I'VE GONE TO LOOK
FOR MYSELF
IF I SHOULD RETURN
BEFORE I GET BACK
PLEASE KEEP ME HERE

Poems by Jeri Lee

ECHOES-
HAVE YOU HEARD THEM
SOUNDS FROM AFAR
ARE THEY WHISPERS FROM
YOU'RE PAST
HOLOGRAMS OF ILLUSIONS
OR PART OF A DREAM.
ARE THEY VIBRATIONS OF MUSIC
FROM THE COSMIC CHOIR
OR LESSONS OF LIFE
IN A REINCARNATED FORM.
JUST OUT OF REACH
OF EXACT KNOWING
ARE THEY JUST A
TANTALIZING FRUSTRATIONS?
THEIR FORMAT IS
FOR THOSE WHO ARE AWARE
LISTEN CLOSELY AND
YOU WILL KNOW
THE TRUTHS THAT
MAKE YOU-YOU

Poems by Jeri Lee

Committed to she who holds my heart
In the warmth of her embrace;
To the one who brings the sunshine
Through the smile upon her face.
Silent moments make me wonder
Of all the questions gone untold,
All the petty secrets not confessed
and with what truth they hold.

Accuse me not. In guilt I stand,
Loving her without demand
But should I fight ambition's bind,
Or let love ease my peace of mind?
Content I'll be if love is born.
Lest my heart become lovelorn:
Then must I fight the gates of hell--
Perchance my love seems trivial.

Renew my heart with love's warm ray
Of whispered love that's here to stay;
Engulf what distance holds apart,
The cherished moments heart to heart.
Yet questions asked should I remain;
For doubts ne'er decked the hall of fame.
Why ground myself, when I can wing
To heights where only robins sing?

Her smile may ne'er meet mine again
Or our past be reemployed;
Our paths may never cross or stay
Filled with chatter of yesterday.
The love she gave I'll cherish and retain
To count our parting no loss, but gain;
With dreams that smile until the day
Our maker takes my last breath away.

Poems by Jeri Lee

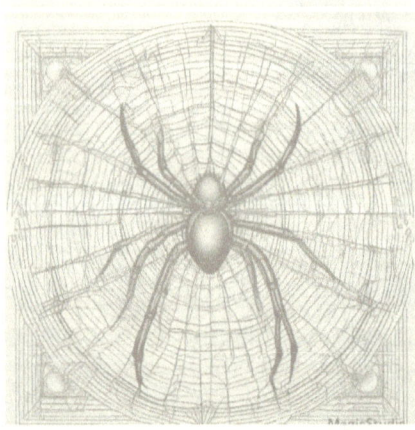

COBWEBS
IN MY BRAIN-
SPIDERWOMAN HAS
SPUN HER TRAP
I NOW VIEW MY WORLD
THROUGH HER DESIGNS
WHAT HAPPENED TO MY
LIFE MAP
WHAT HAPPENED TO MY
DREAMS AND GOALS
DOES IT REALLY MATTER
IS IT IMPORTANT TO
ONLY ME AND OTHERS
NEVER SEE
THAT DEEP WITHIN THIS
WELL OF SELF
I KNOW – YES I KNOW

Poems by Jeri Lee

What is it that hurts you most
That tares apart your heart
and makes you ill beyond control?
The things you can not fix -
That's what.
You patched their wounds
You kissed their tears
You taught them how to care.
For them you were always there
You gave until it hurt.
Now it's your turn
What happens to you?
Forgotten lost and alone
You face your future gloom.
So wash your hands and
Swallow you pride
Then run away from home.

Poems by Jeri Lee

ALONE
Alone is a place
That follows you
Through longings
Never touched
Words never spoken
Scenes never explored
Emotions never conquered
And life never shared
Alone is you
Keeping yourself
From knowing

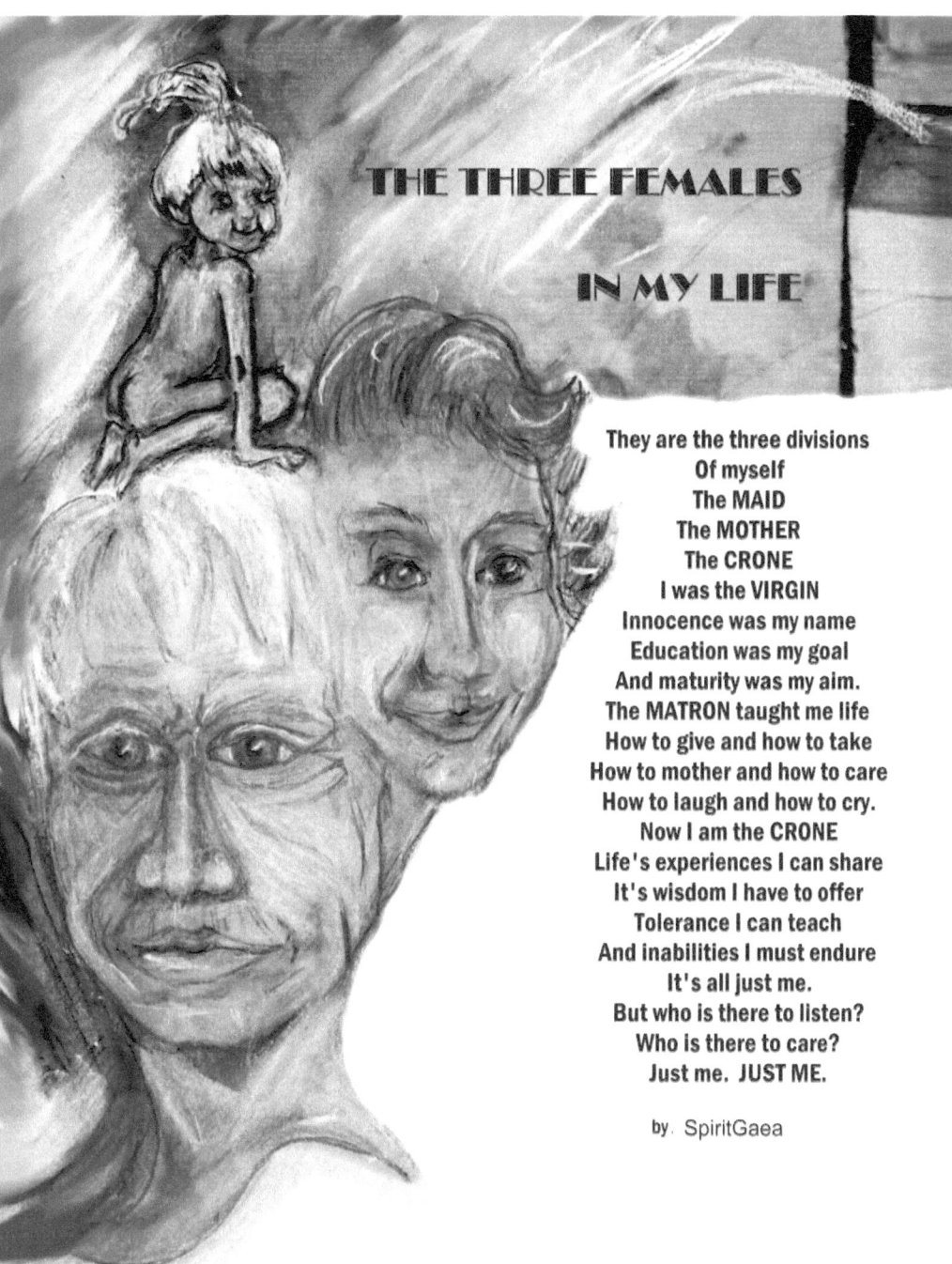

THE THREE FEMALES

IN MY LIFE

They are the three divisions
Of myself
The MAID
The MOTHER
The CRONE
I was the VIRGIN
Innocence was my name
Education was my goal
And maturity was my aim.
The MATRON taught me life
How to give and how to take
How to mother and how to care
How to laugh and how to cry.
Now I am the CRONE
Life's experiences I can share
It's wisdom I have to offer
Tolerance I can teach
And inabilities I must endure
It's all just me.
But who is there to listen?
Who is there to care?
Just me. JUST ME.

by. SpiritGaea

Today

I ate a

RAINBOW
and
I FeeL GREAT

What is Life ?

The whisper of the wind
The babble of the brook
The chirping of the birds
The heartbeat of a loved one
The sound of a tender voice
The touch that sooths all heartache
A smile that gives you bliss
The wisdom of the ages
The truth we all behold
The echo of forever
Our memories seamed in gold
Knock on that door of ages
Enter your dreams and see
Share yourself with others
For life is not, unless you are
So listen to the silent one
The self that dwells within
For it will show you right from wrong
And teach you how to live.

by Jeri Lee

Open Your Mind and Say 'AH'

Universal Peace

Add a little bThe All is one concept of Universal Peace Have you ever said, "The world needs universal peace"? Well I have and many years ago I took it upon myself to make a statement to that effect in symbolic design, and I created the all Is One Cross and the All Is One Star, they symbolize my concept of UNIVERSAL PEACE. As an Artist, Author, Silversmith and Scholas. I spent many years in research and study of Archeology and cultural anthropology specializing in the origin of humans and their beliefs. The first truth is that all humans go back to a single source that was genetically modified and influenced by species of space travelers. Second, is that Astronomy is the elementary science of Astrology and its theology is the original religion. All religions are theologies having the same thread of truth weaving itself through each of them. Whether they are considered modern or ancient their gods are the heroes of their evolution, and their symbols are their signature. Based on this knowledge, I took the symbols of the world's old ancient religions and arranged them into the shape of a cross and into the pentagram to create this beautiful statement of art. I named it "ALL IS ONE" and label is my concept of UNIVERSAL PEACE. Since 1988 I have produced both of these symbols in the form of jewelry and marketing them across the country at Art shows, Renaissance faire, Specialty catalogues and New Age Bookstores. Thank you for reading my letter and may you all strive to make this World a better place to live in.

1 OM The sound of Creation

2 Yin Yang two primal Cosmic forces

3 Triquetra the interlocked ovals of the vesica pisiva

4 Solar Cross Symbol of Earth

5 Pentagram Magick of Wicca Occult

6 Star of David invo;ution of God and evolution of Mon

My Hallmark
is JKL
search on
Ebay

C8 Sir George w\stone Limited Edition

F21 Pendragon

DR7

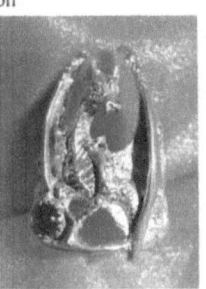

DR9

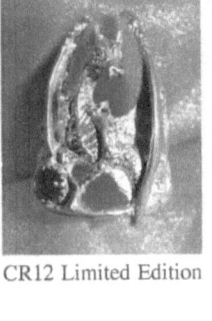

DR5

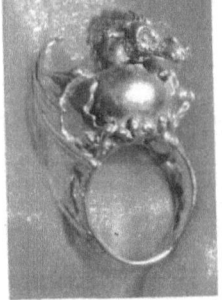

CR12 Limited Edition

DR6

F22 Dragon on skull

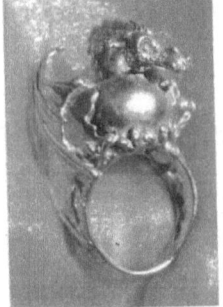

CR4 Limited Edition

DRAGONS

Some say that dragons are the followers of the goddess, and a threat to christianity - therefore they must by destroyed. But some can still be found if you but seek. With ability to fly, the dragon can travel freely between all realms and thus becomes a messenger and possesses many secrets. They are the guardians of the treasures of esoteric knowledge.

DR8

F 7

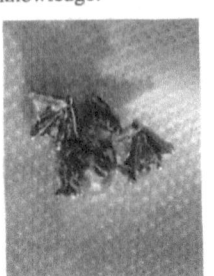

F40 Flying dragon w\stone

F9 & F9-A

F6 thru F6-6
w\stone

Organic casting -it was the real thing

Jewelry by Jeri Lee

L.A. Gay Fairs Before CSW

In addition to Gay symbol jewelry, I carved wax and created unique fantasy art they bought and proudly sported. The highlight of my castings was casting real creatures from nature, such as lizards, frogs, snakes, and turtles. Also, sand dollars, crabs, and sea horses. I was known as the lizard lady due to the bracelet I cast for myself and wore continuously. I will include a photo; perhaps you will remember seeing it and knowing we have met.

My Black Cat and the Lizard

It was somewhere around 1985 and we were doing a Street show in San Francisco California. Across from us was a booth occupied by the SPCA giving away homeless animals. My partner, the K in JKL, cruised their booth and came back with the little black kitten.

I was holding the kitten and introducing myself to her when a black lady came up to my booth. After observing my actions for several minutes she made one comment and then walked off. Looking me straight in the eye she said, "I hope you know that all Black Cats are crazy."

Well, we added the kitten to our pack making the 13th cat in our house and called her Hackett. She grew up to be a beautiful specimen of our witches familiar. At that time our home was located on four acres of desert with a guesthouse that was rented to a lady with two children and the cat would bring presents to me at night from the children's play yard and leave them in the middle of the living room. I told her one night if you're going to steal things, mug an old lady and bring me some jewels, so she did, she went into my shop and bought bags of my jewelry and left them in the living room.

Then in the middle of the winter I got an order for a lizard bracelet like the one I wore. All lizards were in hibernation by now so there were none running around the yard for my kids to catch.

So I sit down on the floor with this black cat and I explained to her that we needed money to feed the family and in order to do that I had to produce this bracelet and I showed her my bracelet so she could see the size of the lizard and the species and told her that she had to go out in the desert and find me a lizard.

Well, next morning she was standing at the sliding glass door, belly to the glass, flailing both arms, with a lizard hanging from her mouth. It was in hibernation still and it was the exact species, and the exact size as the lizard on my bracelet.

This is a true story== believe it or not == I believe the black lady was correct but they weren't only crazy they're intelligent.

Save the Planet

Coloring Books

8.5 x 11 100 pages

Jeri Lee

Mother Earth

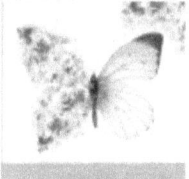

on Amazon
by
Jeri Lee C. HT.

Family Pets

Color Your
Tarot Cards

ChineseCrested.US

Art Nouveau   Classic   Best in show   So Cute

Vacation   Walk in the park   Competition   Bewitched

I'm not Ugly   Art Deco   Queen 4 a Day   Zodiac

In Drag   Zodiac - Do I have to - I'm not a Gremlin

The Devil made   Puppies R US   MotherDay   Rainbow

**More Books
by Jeri Lee**

**Find them on
Amazon**

About the Author
Jeri Lee C.Ht.

I Died
Twice BUT

REFUSED to
Stay DEAD

Born on May 1, 1939 I was a Beltane child that was destine to be involved in the Esoteric world. I met the Tarot in 1971 and have been it's student since. It teaches you life and how to live it - if you take time to listen to yourself. In 1985 I died but refused to stay dead and then repeat it in 2005. This is 2025 and I am now 86 and hesitate answering the door as death knocks. If you want to know how I did this I tell my story in my book 'Twice I refused to Stay Dead'

the First Gay Pride Parade   Jeri Lee

If You Enjoyed my
true story
Please Give Me a Positive Review

Thank You

Poetry
from my
Dreams

Homosexual LOVE

Jeri Lee C.Ht.